· LITTLE HOUSE ·

The Laura Years

❖ ❖ ❖

Little House Chapter Books are written for children who want to share in the adventures of everyone's favorite pioneer girl, Laura Ingalls, but who are not quite ready for the classic Little House novels. Little House Chapter Books are gentle adaptations of Laura Ingalls Wilder's original books, enhanced by beautiful black-and-white illustrations created by Renée Graef in Garth Williams' beloved Little House style.

❖ ❖ ❖

THE LITTLE HOUSE
CHAPTER BOOKS
Adapted from the Little House books
by Laura Ingalls Wilder
Illustrated by Renée Graef

Little House Friends

Adapted from the Little House books by
LAURA INGALLS WILDER

illustrated by
RENÉE GRAEF

HarperTrophy®
A Division of HarperCollinsPublishers

Adaptation by Heather Henson.

Illustrations for this book are inspired by the work of Garth Williams with his permission, which we gratefully acknowledge.

HarperCollins®, ☎®, Harper Trophy®, Little House®, and The Laura Years™ are trademarks of HarperCollins Publishers Inc.

Library of Congress Cataloging-in-Publication Data
Little house friends : [adapted from the Little house books by Laura Ingalls Wilder] / illustrated by Renée Graef.
    p.   cm. — (A Little house chapter book)
    Summary: Laura Ingalls shares adventures and good times with her friends while growing up on the western frontier.
    ISBN 0-06-027894-3. — ISBN 0-06-442080-9 (pbk.)
    1. Wilder, Laura Ingalls, 1867–1957—Juvenile fiction. [1. Wilder, Laura Ingalls, 1867–1957—Fiction. 2. Friendship—Fiction. 3. Frontier and pioneer life—Fiction.] I. Wilder, Laura Ingalls, 1867–1957. II. Graef, Renée, ill. III. Series.
PZ7.L7347 1998   97-39280
[Fic]—dc21   CIP
                                                                                   AC

◆
First Harper Trophy edition, 1998
Reprinted by arrangement with HarperCollins Publishers.
10 9 8 7 6 5

Contents

CHAPTER 1

Laura and Lena

When Laura first saw Lena, she knew she would like her. Lena's eyes were black and snappy. Her curly hair was black as black could be.

"Do you like to ride horseback?" Lena asked Laura right away. "We've got two black ponies. I can drive them all by myself. Tomorrow I'm going for the washing. You can come too, if you want to. Do you?"

"Yes!" said Laura.

Lena was Laura's cousin. She was one year older than Laura, and she had a little brother named Jean. Lena and Jean lived with Uncle Hi and Aunt Docia in a railroad camp in Dakota Territory.

Uncle Hi worked for the railroad. Laura's Pa had come to help him. Laura and her sisters, Mary, Carrie, and baby Grace, and their Ma and Pa had traveled all the way from Minnesota to Dakota Territory. They were staying with Uncle Hi and Aunt Docia until they found a place of their own.

Uncle Hi and Aunt Docia's little house was so crowded, there was no room for Laura and Lena. They had to sleep in a tent.

After supper, Lena took Laura outside. The tent looked small under the big black sky. It seemed far away from the warm, cozy house.

When Laura peeked inside, she saw that the tent was empty. There was only a blanket spread over the grass on the ground. Laura felt a little lost and lonesome. She didn't think she would like sleeping on the ground in a tent. She wished Ma and Pa were there.

Lena thought it was great fun to sleep in the tent. She flopped down right away.

"Don't we undress?" Laura asked sleepily. She was very tired. It had been a long journey from their little house on the banks of Plum Creek in Minnesota. Now she was far away, in a strange new place.

"What for?" Lena asked. "You only have to put on your clothes again in the morning. Besides, there aren't any covers."

So Laura lay down beside Lena. She closed her eyes, and in no time at all, it was morning.

Sunshine coming through the tent woke Laura. She opened her eyes just as

3

Lena opened hers. The girls looked at each other and laughed.

"Hurry up!" Lena sang out. "We're going for the washing!"

Since they hadn't undressed, there was no need to dress.

Laura and Lena jumped up and ran outside. The sun was shining, and the prairie stretched out as far as Laura could see. There were two black ponies grazing in the tall prairie grass. Their shining manes and tails were blowing in the wind.

"We've got to eat breakfast first," Lena said. "Come on, Laura! Hurry!"

They raced inside the house. Everyone was already at the table. Aunt Docia was frying pancakes.

Aunt Docia cooked for all the men in the railroad camp. There were so many meals to cook, and so many dishes to wash, that Aunt Docia and Lena were busy every day from sunrise to sunset. There was never any time for them to wash their clothes. So Aunt Docia had hired a homesteader's wife to do it for her.

The homesteaders lived three miles away. It was Lena's job to drive the buggy to pick up the washing.

After breakfast, Lena untied the black ponies from their picket lines. Laura helped her harness them to the buggy. Lena and Laura climbed up, and Lena took the reins.

Pa had never let Laura drive his horses. He said she was not strong enough to hold them if they ran away.

As soon as Lena took the reins, the black ponies began to trot. The buggy wheels turned quickly, and the prairie wind blew. Faster and faster went the ponies. Faster went the wheels. Laura and Lena laughed with joy.

The trotting ponies touched noses, gave a little squeal, and started to run.

Up sailed the buggy, and Laura almost bounced out of the seat. Her bonnet flapped behind her. She held on to the edge of the seat. The ponies were stretched out low, running with all their might.

"They're running away!" Laura cried.

"Let 'em run!" Lena shouted. "They can't run against anything but grass!" And then Lena yelled to the ponies, "Hi! Yi! Yi, yi, yee-ee!"

The ponies' long black manes and tails streamed behind them. Their feet pounded and the buggy sailed. Everything went rushing by too fast to be seen.

"Hi, yi, yi, yi yipee-ee!" Lena and Laura called together. But the ponies couldn't go any faster. They were going as fast as they could.

"I guess I better breathe them," Lena said. She pulled and pulled until she made the ponies trot. Then they slowed down to a walk. Everything seemed quiet and slow.

"I wish I could drive," Laura said. "I always wanted to, but Pa won't let me."

"You can drive a ways," Lena offered.

Just then the ponies touched noses, squealed, and ran.

"You can drive on the way home!" Lena promised.

Singing and whooping, they went racing on across the prairie. Every time Lena slowed the ponies, they got their breath back and ran again. In no time at all, they reached the homesteaders' little one-room house.

The homesteader's wife came out to the buggy. She carried a heavy basket of washing. Her face and arms and bare feet were brown as leather from the sun.

Lena talked to the homesteader's wife for a while, and then she tugged on the reins. Soon Laura and Lena were far out in the middle of the prairie again.

"May I drive now?" Laura asked.

 8

Lena gave her the reins. "All you have to do is hold on," Lena said. "The ponies know the way back."

At that instant, the ponies touched noses and squealed.

"Hold on to them, Laura! Hold on to them!" Lena screeched.

Laura braced her feet and hung on to the reins with all her might. She could feel that the ponies didn't mean any harm. They were running because they wanted to run.

Laura hung on and yelled, "Yi, yi, yi, yip-ee!"

When they were nearly home, the girls looked down. They had forgotten the basket of clothes!

Back across the prairie they raced, whooping and singing. The ponies went running, trotting, and running again.

It was almost noon when they finally came home. Laura and Lena climbed out of the buggy and unhitched the ponies. Then they saw that some of the clean clothes had blown out onto the buggy floor and were under the seats.

Guiltily, they picked up the clothes and smoothed them out as best they could. Together they lugged the heavy basket into the house.

Ma and Aunt Docia were dishing up the dinner.

"You girls look as if butter wouldn't melt in your mouths," said Aunt Docia. "What have you been up to?"

"Why, we just drove out and brought back the washing," Lena said.

Laura and Lena looked at each other and smiled. Laura couldn't wait to drive the fast black ponies again.

CHAPTER 2

The Black Ponies

That afternoon was even more exciting than the morning. As soon as the dinner dishes were washed, Lena and Laura ran outside to the ponies.

One of the ponies was gone. Jean had taken it. They saw him riding away across the prairie.

"No fair!" Lena yelled.

The other pony was galloping in a circle around its picket line. Lena grabbed its mane and unsnapped the rope. She sailed right up onto the back of the running pony.

Laura watched Lena and Jean race in circles. Their hair streamed back and their hands clutched the flying black manes. Their brown legs clasped the ponies' sides. The ponies curved and swerved, chasing each other on the prairie like birds in the sky. Laura loved watching them.

The ponies came galloping up and stopped in front of Laura. Lena and Jean slid off.

"Come on, Laura," Lena said. "You can ride Jean's pony."

Laura took hold of the pony's mane. The pony was much bigger than she was. It was tall and strong.

"I don't know if I can," said Laura.

"I'll put you on," Lena said. She bent down and held her hand out for Laura to step onto.

Laura still wasn't sure. The pony

seemed bigger every minute. It was strong enough to hurt her if it wanted to. It was so high that if Laura fell off, she might break a bone. She was so scared to ride that pony that she knew she had to try.

Laura stepped onto Lena's hand and scrambled up. The pony's body was warm and slippery. Laura got one leg over the pony's back, and then everything began to move very fast.

"Hang on to his mane," Lena cried.

Laura *was* holding on to the pony's mane. She was holding on to deep handfuls of it with all her might. Her elbows and her knees were holding on to the pony, too. But she was jolting so much, it was hard to think.

The ground was so far away that Laura didn't dare look down. Every second she was falling. But then, before she really fell, she was falling the other way. The jolting rattled her teeth.

She heard Lena yell from far off, "Hang on, Laura!"

Then everything smoothed out to a steady motion. Laura and the pony were sailing through the rushing air. Laura opened her eyes. She saw the pony's black mane blowing and her hands holding it. She was flying, and nothing could happen to her until she stopped.

Lena's pony came pounding along beside her.

Laura wanted to ask how to stop, but she could not speak. She saw the houses far ahead. She knew that somehow the ponies had turned around. They were headed back toward camp.

The jolting began again. Then it

stopped. And there Laura sat on the pony's back.

"Didn't I tell you it's fun?" said Lena.

"What makes it jolt so?" Laura asked.

"That's trotting," Lena told her. "You don't want to trot. You want to make your pony gallop. Just yell at it, like I did. Come on, let's go a long ways this time. You want to?"

"Yes," said Laura.

"All right, hang on," said Lena. "Now, yell!"

All day they rode the black ponies back and forth across the prairie.

That was a wonderful afternoon. Laura fell off twice. Once the pony's head hit her nose and made it bleed. But Laura never let go of the mane.

Laura's braids came undone and her throat grew sore from laughing and screeching. Her legs were scratched from running through the sharp grass and trying to leap onto her pony while it was running. She almost could, but not quite.

Lena and Jean always swung up onto the running ponies. They raced each other, trying to see who could get on the pony the fastest.

Laura and Lena and Jean were having so much fun, they did not hear Aunt Docia calling them to supper. They did not hear until Pa came out and told them to come inside.

When they came into the house, Ma looked at Laura in surprise.

"Really, Docia," Ma said, "I don't know when Laura's looked so wild."

"She and Lena are a pair," Aunt Docia agreed.

CHAPTER 3

New Friends

Laura loved playing with Lena on the big open prairie. She wished that she and Lena could ride the black ponies forever. But then Pa's railroad job ended. It was time for the railroad workers and their families to move on. First Lena moved away, and then Laura moved.

Pa said that Dakota winters were long and hard. He had built them a little house in the town of De Smet where they would stay snug and warm. Laura wasn't sure she would like moving to town and living near so many other people.

Living in town meant that Laura and her sister Carrie would be going to a new school. Laura's older sister, Mary, would not be going to school with them. Back in Minnesota, Mary had caught scarlet fever, and the fever had left her blind. Although she could no longer see, Mary still did lessons in her head. And she helped Ma at home by taking care of baby Grace.

Laura was sorry Mary could not go to school with her, but she also knew she could teach Mary the lessons she learned. And at school, there would be new friends to play with.

On the first morning of school, Laura and Carrie walked through town. The early-morning sun was shining. The store-keepers were sweeping out their stores.

Carrie took hold of Laura's hand as they walked. Laura had been to school before, but Carrie had not. Laura was always shy when she had to meet new people. Somehow, it made her feel better to hold Carrie's hand. She would have to be brave for Carrie.

They crossed Main Street and walked along Second Street. It seemed like a long walk to the schoolhouse.

Laura saw a group of boys playing ball in front of the schoolhouse. Two girls were standing by the schoolhouse door.

One of the girls was tall and dark. She had smooth black hair, and her blue dress was longer than Laura's brown one. Laura felt shy all over again.

Just then, one of the boys leaped into the air to catch a ball. He was tall and quick and moved like a cat. His yellow hair was almost white, and his eyes were blue. He saw Laura, and a big grin flashed across his face. He threw the ball to her.

Before she could think, Laura made a running jump and caught the ball. A great shout went up from the other boys.

"Hey, Cap!" they cried. "Girls don't play ball!"

"She's as good as any of us!" Cap shouted. "Come on and play," he said to Laura. Then he called to the other girls,

"Come on, Mary Power and Minnie! You play with us too!"

But Laura threw back the ball, picked up the books she had dropped, and took Carrie's hand. They walked on to the schoolhouse door. Laura knew the other girls didn't play ball with the boys. She wondered what they would think of her.

"I'm Mary Power," the dark girl said, "and this is Minnie Johnson."

Minnie Johnson was thin and fair and pale. She had freckles.

"I'm Laura Ingalls," Laura said, "and this is my little sister Carrie."

Mary Power's eyes were blue, and her lashes were long and black. She smiled at Laura, and Laura smiled back.

"That was Cap Garland who threw you the ball," Mary Power said.

 22

There was no time to say anything else. The teacher came to the door and rang the bell. It was time for school to begin.

The girls sat on one side of the room and the boys sat on the other. They had all been coming to school for a week and knew where to sit. Laura and Carrie did not.

"You're new, aren't you?" the teacher asked Laura in a kind voice. She told Laura to take a seat in back, across the aisle from Mary Power. And she told Carrie to sit up front with the little girls.

Every day, Laura liked school a little bit more. She did not have a seatmate, but at recess and at noontimes, she and Mary Power and Minnie Johnson sat together and talked. Sometimes they watched the boys play ball.

There was brown-eyed, dark-haired Ben Woodworth, who lived at the railroad depot. There was Minnie's brother, Arthur Johnson. He was thin and fair just like his sister. Cap Garland was the strongest and quickest. He would spring high into the air to catch the ball. He had a big grin that made other people smile too.

After school, Laura always walked home with her new friends. When Saturdays came, she was almost sad. She couldn't wait until Monday to see Mary Power and Minnie again.

But one day, a blizzard hit the little town. All day and all night, it snowed. No one could go outdoors, and school was closed.

Laura had never seen such a blizzard. Wind shook the little house. The windows were thick with furry white frost. The whole family stayed close by the kitchen stove to keep warm. It snowed for three days. Laura thought it would never stop snowing.

Then one day it did stop. Pa told them there would be school that day. Laura and Carrie put on their school dresses in the warm kitchen and bundled into their coats.

When they went outside, it was icy cold but the sun was shining. The whole outdoors sparkled in the bright sunshine.

Main Street was one big snowdrift! The snowdrift was taller than Laura. They had to climb up one side and down the other to get to school.

In the school yard, there was another snowdrift. It was almost as high as the schoolhouse. Cap Garland and Ben and Arthur were all skating down it on their shoes. Mary Power and Minnie were standing out in the cold sunshine watch-ing the boys.

"Hello, Laura!" Mary Power called. She was wearing warm woolen mittens. She tucked her hand under Laura's arm and squeezed. Laura smiled. She was glad to be with her friends again.

Laura and Mary and Minnie stood together, watching the boys slide down the big snowdrift. Laura wished she could play too.

"I don't think it's any fun being a big girl," Laura said at last.

"We can't help growing up," Mary Power answered.

But after school, even the big girls went racing and shouting over the tall snowdrift on Main Street. They all climbed to the top. Some slid one way and some slid the other.

Laura and Carrie called good-by to their friends and slid right down to their own front door.

Laura loved playing in the snow, but she was glad the blizzard was over. It was good to see the town alive again and to know that again all the weekdays would be school days.

CHAPTER 4

Nellie Comes
to Town

The days grew warmer, and soon the school year ended. Summer came and went. Before they knew it, Laura and Carrie were setting out for another first day of school. They wore their best calico dresses, and they carried their schoolbooks under their arms.

Main Street was growing longer. New families were moving west, and so the little town was getting bigger every day.

As Laura and Carrie came closer to

the school yard, they saw a large crowd of children. The boys stood on one side, and the girls stood on the other. Many of them were strangers. There must have been twenty boys and girls.

Laura's knees began to shake a little when she saw so many new faces. She felt like turning around and running home. Then she saw Mary Power and Minnie Johnson in the crowd.

"Hello, Laura," Mary called.

Mary's dark eyes were glad to see Laura. So was Minnie's freckled face. Laura felt better right away. She knew she would always like Mary and Minnie.

The teacher rang the bell, and they all went into the schoolhouse. Laura took her seat in the back near Mary and Minnie. Carrie sat up front nearer to the teacher with the smaller girls.

When Laura looked up, she saw a girl standing all alone in the aisle. She seemed about the same age as Laura. And she looked just as shy. The girl glanced timidly at Laura.

Laura smiled and patted the seat beside her. The girl's brown eyes lit up. She laid her books on the desk and sat down beside Laura.

All the students had taken their places. The teacher was ready to begin school when the door opened again. Everyone turned to see who was tardy on the first day.

Laura could not believe her eyes. It was Nellie Oleson.

Laura had known Nellie when she lived in Plum Creek, Minnesota. Nellie had made fun of Laura because Laura was a country girl and Nellie was a town girl.

 30

She had been rude to Ma and mean to Laura's good old bulldog, Jack.

Laura looked at Nellie. She was taller now, and prettier. But Laura could see that Nellie still held her nose high. Her mouth was still prim and prissy.

"I would like a back seat, if you please," Nellie said to the teacher.

Then Nellie looked right at Laura.

She gave Laura a look that said, "Get out and give me that seat."

Laura sat firmly at her desk. She looked right back at Nellie.

Finally Nellie's eyes looked away. She nodded at Minnie's seat and said, "That place will do."

"Will you change for our new girl, Minnie?" the teacher asked.

It wasn't fair! The teacher had already let Minnie sit there.

"Yes, ma'am," Minnie answered quietly. Slowly she picked up her books and went to the empty seat in the next row.

Then Mary stood up.

"I'll go with Minnie," she said.

Nellie sat down smiling. She had come to school late, but she had gotten the best seat in the room. And she had a whole desk to herself.

Laura was mad. But then she felt better when she heard Nellie tell the teacher that her family lived on a farm outside of town. Nellie was a country girl now!

At recess, all the girls stayed together. Laura talked to her new seatmate. Her name was Ida Brown, and she was as friendly as she looked. She had soft brown eyes, and her hair was black and wavy. Laura liked her.

But Nellie wanted all the attention for herself.

"I don't know whether we'll like it out here," Nellie said. "We're from the east. We're not used to such a rough country and rough people."

"You come from Plum Creek, from the same place we did," Laura said.

"Oh, *that*!" said Nellie. "We were there

only a little while. We come from the east. From New York State."

"We all come from the east," Mary Power told her. "Come on, let's go outside in the sunshine."

"My goodness, no!" said Nellie. "Why, this wind will tan your skin!"

Laura looked around. They were all tan but Nellie. Her face was pale, and her hands were slim and white. Laura could not imagine Nellie doing farm work.

There was no time to go outside anyway. Recess was over. The teacher came to the door and rang the bell.

At home that night, Carrie talked and talked about the day at school, but Laura was quiet.

"Anything go wrong at school today, Laura?" Pa asked gently.

So Laura told Pa and Ma about Nellie

Oleson and all she had said and done.

"I don't know how it happened, but Mr. Oleson lost everything he had in Minnesota," Pa said. "He hasn't a thing in the world now but his farm."

"But Nellie has such pretty clothes," Laura said. "And she can't do a bit of work. She keeps her face and hands so white."

"You could wear your sunbonnet, you know," said Ma. "And Nellie may have nice clothes, but perhaps that's all she has."

Laura didn't say anything. She knew Ma wanted her to be sorry for Nellie, but she wasn't. She wished that Nellie Oleson had stayed in Plum Creek.

CHAPTER 5

Candy at Recess

The weather was turning cold again. At recess and at noontime, the boys still played baseball. But Laura and her friends stayed inside the schoolhouse. Nellie worked at her crocheting. Ida and Minnie and Mary Power stood at the window and talked and watched the boys play ball.

Sometimes Laura stood with them, but sometimes she stayed at her desk and studied. She needed to study hard. Pa and Ma wanted her to be a teacher when she grew up.

"Oh, come on, Laura," Ida coaxed one day. "Come join us. You have a long time to study before you need to know so much."

Laura closed her book. She was happy that the girls wanted her.

Nellie tossed her head. "I'm glad I don't have to be a teacher," she said. "My folks will be able to get along without my having to work."

Laura was mad. She thought about what Pa had told her about Nellie's father losing everything he had. She wanted to say something mean back to Nellie.

Mary spoke up. "Laura will be a good teacher," she said.

"Yes, she will," said Ida.

Just then, the door opened and Cap Garland came inside. He was holding a small striped paper bag.

37

"Hello, girls," he said. He looked at Mary Power, and a big grin lit up his whole face. He held the bag out to her.

"Have some candy?" he asked.

But Nellie was too quick. She grabbed the bag from Cap's hand and smiled up at him. "Oh, Cappie!" she said sweetly. "How did you know that I like candy so much?"

Cap's eyes opened wide. He didn't know what to say. Everybody knew that Cap liked Mary Power. He had brought the candy for her.

"Would you girls like some?" Nellie asked. She held the bag out to the other girls but then quickly stuck it into her skirt pocket.

The next day at noon, Cap brought candy again. Again, he tried to give the candy to Mary Power. But again, Nellie was too quick.

"Oh Cappie, it's so nice of you to bring me more candy," she said, smiling her sweet smile.

Cap didn't know what to do. He was too nice to tell Nellie that the candy wasn't for her. And Mary Power was too proud to say anything.

Nellie turned away from the other girls. Laura watched her eat all the candy herself, and she remembered what a selfish little girl Nellie had been in Plum Creek.

Back then, Nellie's father had been a storekeeper. Mary and Laura had gone to his store to buy a slate. Nellie had walked right past them to a tall wooden barrel. She had dug her hands deep into the barrel and come up with two fistfuls of candy. She had stared right at Mary and Laura as she crammed the candy into her mouth. She hadn't offered them a single piece. When Mary and Laura were leaving, Nellie had stuck out her tongue. It was streaked red and green from the candy.

Nellie was a big girl now. But she was still selfish. It seemed to Laura that she always got her way. Laura wondered what she could do.

The next day, Cap brought candy again. Just as Nellie reached for the bag, Laura stuck out her hand. She took the bag of candy and gave it to Mary Power.

Everyone was startled. Even Laura was surprised at what she had done. But when she looked at Cap, he gave her his big grin.

Then Cap looked at Mary to see what she would do. Mary smiled at Cap, and Cap grinned back.

"Thank you," Mary said to him. "We'll all enjoy the candy so much."

And she held the bag out for the other girls to share.

CHAPTER 6

Name Cards

"Will you write in my autograph album?" Laura asked Mary Power one day.

Mary Power smiled and sat down at her desk. She took a pen and began to carefully write in Laura's album.

All the girls had autograph albums except Nellie. At recess and at noontime, they wrote in each other's albums. First they copied a special poem onto a page of the album, and then they signed their names.

Laura's autograph album had a red

cover with gold lettering on the front. The blank pages were all different soft colors. Ma said autograph albums were what all the big girls had back east.

When Mary was finished, Laura looked at the page. Mary's handwriting was beautiful, and so was the little poem she had chosen to put down.

Then Minnie Johnson asked Laura to write in her autograph album.

"I will, if you'll write in mine," Laura said.

"I'll do my best, but I can't write as beautifully as Mary does," Minnie said.

Minnie sat down and wrote:

When the name that I write here
Is dim on the page
And the leaves of your album
Are yellow with age,

Still think of me kindly
And do not forget
That wherever I am
I remember you yet.
           Minnie Johnson.

Laura smiled when she saw the poem. She had so many new friends. Soon her autograph album would be full.

That afternoon at recess, Nellie sneered at Laura when she brought out her album again.

"Autograph albums are out of date," Nellie said. "I used to have one, but I wouldn't have one of those old things now."

Laura didn't believe her. Autograph albums could not be out of style, because Laura's was almost new.

"In the east, where I come from," said

 44

Nellie, "everyone has name cards now."

"What are name cards?" Ida asked.

Nellie pretended to be surprised. Then she smiled.

"Well, of course you wouldn't know," she said. "I'll bring mine to school and show you. But I won't give you one, because you don't have one to give me. It's only proper to *exchange* name cards. Everybody's exchanging name cards now in the east."

Laura still did not believe her.

On the way home from school that day, Minnie said, "Nellie's just bragging. I don't believe she has name cards. I don't believe there's any such thing."

But early the next morning, Mary Power and Minnie were waiting for Laura outside her house. Mary Power had found out about name cards.

They were colored cards with pictures of flowers and birds on them. Mr. Hopp was selling them in his newspaper office. You picked out the color and the picture you liked, and then Mr. Hopp printed your name on the cards.

"I don't believe Nellie has any," Minnie said. "She just found out about them before we did. She's only pretending they came from the east."

"How much do they cost?" Laura asked.

"Twenty-five cents for twelve," Mary Power answered. "My father said I could get some."

Laura said no more. Mary Power's father was the tailor. He could afford to give Mary twenty-five cents. Laura could never ask Pa for that kind of money.

As soon as they got to school, Minnie

asked Nellie if she had brought her name cards.

"My goodness, I forgot all about them," Nellie said. "I guess I'll have to tie a string on my finger to remind me."

Minnie looked at Mary Power and Laura. "I told you so," she whispered.

The next week, Mary Power brought her name cards to school. They were beautiful. They were pale green. In the middle was a pretty little picture of a bird. Under the picture, MARY POWER was printed in black letters.

Mary gave one to Minnie and one to Ida and one to Laura even though they had none to give her.

That same day, Nellie brought hers to school. They were pale yellow, with a bouquet of flowers. Her name was printed in letters that looked like handwriting.

Nellie traded one of her cards for one of Mary's. She did not give any to the other girls.

The next day, Minnie said she was going to buy some. Her father had given her the money. She asked Laura and Mary Power to come with her after school to pick them out.

Laura tried not to be jealous. She wished she could have name cards of her very own. But she knew she could not ask Pa.

After school, Laura and Mary and Minnie went to the newspaper office. Mr. Hopp spread the name cards out on the counter for the girls to see.

Each card was more beautiful than the last. They were all in delicate pale colors. Some had golden edges, and there were all kinds of flowers and birds to choose from.

One card had two birds sitting inside a bird's nest. The word Love was written across the top.

Laura knew it was mean of her, but she was happy to see one of Nellie's cards among the samples. It proved that Nellie had bought her cards there.

The girls looked at the cards all afternoon. It was so hard to choose. Finally, Minnie pointed to a pale-blue one.

When Laura came home, Ma was already putting supper on the table.

"Where have you been, Laura?" Ma asked.

"I'm sorry, Ma," Laura said. She told them about the beautiful name cards. Of course she did not say she wanted one.

Later that night, when it was almost bedtime, Pa folded his newspaper.

"Laura," he said.

"Yes, Pa?"

"You want some of these new-fangled name cards, don't you?" Pa asked.

"I was just thinking the same thing, Charles," Ma said.

"Well, yes, I do want them," Laura said slowly. "But I don't *need* them."

Pa's eyes twinkled. He reached into his pocket and took out some coins. He counted out two dimes and one nickel.

"I guess you can have them, Half-Pint," he said. "Here you are."

Laura could hardly speak.

"Oh, Pa, *thank you!*" she said at last.

The next day, Laura went by herself to pick out her name cards. Mr. Hopp promised the cards would be ready on Wednesday at noon.

That day, Laura was so excited, she

could hardly eat. At noon she rushed to the newspaper office.

There they were, her delicate pink cards. In the middle was a bouquet of pinker roses and blue cornflowers. Under the bouquet, her name was printed in thin, clear type: Laura Elizabeth Ingalls.

Laura hurried on to school. She couldn't wait to give her new cards to her friends.

CHAPTER 7

The Birthday Party

That school year had already been a wonderful time for Laura and her friends. And now there was going to be a party. It was Ben Woodworth's birthday. He had asked Laura and all the other big girls and boys to come.

For a whole week, Laura thought of nothing but the party. She wanted to go, and she did not want to go. She was excited and scared at the same time.

Laura hadn't been to a party since she was a little girl. And that party had not been much fun. It had been Nellie's party, and Nellie had been mean to Laura.

But Nellie was not coming to this party. The party was going to be in the evening, and Nellie could not come all the way into town from the country.

On the night of the party, Laura put on her Sunday-best dress. She styled her hair in a coiled braid that covered the whole back of her head. Then she sat in the front room and waited for Mary Power. They were going to walk to Ben's house together.

Laura could hardly sit still as she waited. She looked out the window. Mary was nowhere in sight.

"Sit down and wait quietly, Laura," Ma said gently.

Just then, Laura saw Mary. Quickly, she pulled on her coat and her hood and rushed outside.

Laura and Mary hardly spoke as they walked. Laura knew that Mary was just as nervous as she was.

When they reached Ben's house, they saw that the upstairs windows were shining brightly. Mary knocked on the front door.

"Good evening," Ben said when he opened the door. He was wearing his

Sunday suit and a stiff white collar. His hair was damp and carefully combed.

Laura and Mary followed Ben silently. At the top of the stairs, Ben's mother was waiting for them. She wore a soft gray dress with snowy white ruffles at her throat and wrists. She was plump and friendly. Laura felt better right away.

Mrs. Woodworth told them to take off their coats and go into the sitting room. Ida and Minnie, Arthur and Cap and Ben, were already there.

The sitting room was warm and cozy. There were pretty shaded lamps and dark-red curtains at the windows. The chairs were gathered around the stove. The coals glowed red through the stove's door.

When Laura looked around, she saw a plush photograph album sitting on a table with a marble top. There were other books nearby. Laura longed to sit quietly and look at those books, but she knew it would be rude not to talk to the others.

As soon as all the boys and girls were settled in their seats, everything went quiet. No one said a word. Laura knew she should say something, but she couldn't think of anything to say. She looked down at her feet. They seemed much too big. She did not know what to do with her hands.

Laura glanced at the other girls. None of them knew what to say, either. Laura's heart sank. She wondered if all parties were this uncomfortable.

Suddenly, they heard the sound of footsteps springing up the stairs. Ben's older brother, Jim, came bursting into the room. He looked around at them all sitting so quietly, and he started to laugh.

Then they all laughed, too. After that they were able to talk.

When supper was ready, Mrs. Woodworth called them into the dining room. The room was beautiful. China and silver sparkled on a crisp white tablecloth. A glass lamp hung from the ceiling on long golden chains.

At the long table, there were eight plates. The plates were white china with tiny flowers around the edges. Beside each plate was a stiff white napkin, folded to look like a large flower.

Best of all, there was an orange in front of each plate. Each orange had been cut to look like a flower too. Its red-gold peel curled away from the plump center of the orange. Laura's mouth watered just looking at it.

Mrs. Woodworth told them all where to sit. Now Laura's feet were under the table and her hands had something to do. It was all so bright and cheerful that she no longer felt shy.

Mrs. Woodworth had set on each plate a bowl of steaming hot soup. She passed around a bowl of crackers to go with the soup.

The soup was delicious. When they had all eaten every last drop of it, Mrs. Woodworth took their bowls away. She came back from the kitchen carrying big platters piled high with more good things to eat.

Mrs. Woodworth told them all to take seconds. When they had eaten as much as they could, she cleared the table.

Laura thought that would be all. Everything had tasted so good. But then Mrs.

Woodworth came back with a white-frosted birthday cake. She set it down in front of Ben.

Ben stood up to cut the cake. He put one slice on each plate, and Mrs. Woodworth handed the plates around. They all waited until Ben had cut his own slice of cake.

Laura wondered about the orange in front of her. She didn't know if she was supposed to eat it or not. She had eaten only part of an orange once before. She couldn't imagine having a whole orange to herself.

Everyone took a bite of cake, but no one touched an orange. Laura thought that maybe they were supposed to take their oranges home. Then she could share hers with Pa, Ma, Mary, Carrie, and Grace.

Just then, Ben took his orange. He held it carefully over his plate. He peeled it and broke it into its sections. He took a bite from one section; then he took a bite of cake.

Laura reached for her orange, and so did everyone else. Carefully they all divided their oranges into sections just as Ben had done. Laura took a bite of orange and then a bite of cake. The sweet cake and the tangy orange tasted good together.

When she was finished eating, Laura remembered to wipe her lips daintily with her napkin and fold it, just as Ma had taught her to do.

"Now we'll go downstairs and play games," Ben said.

The room downstairs was warm from the stove and bright with light from the lamps. It was big enough to play the liveliest games. First they played drop-the-handkerchief. Then they played blind-man's buff.

Just when they sat down for a minute to catch their breath, they heard the big clock begin to strike ten. Then the door opened and in walked Pa.

"Is the party over?" he asked with a smile. "I've come to see my girl home."

They were all very surprised. None of them had noticed how late it was. And none of them wanted the party to end.

The girls went upstairs to thank Mrs. Woodworth. They buttoned their coats and tied on their hoods.

"Oh! What a good time we had!" Laura and Minnie and Mary all cried at once.

When Laura and Pa got home, Ma was waiting up. Mary and Carrie and Grace were already asleep.

"I can see you had a good time because your eyes are shining," Ma said. "Now slip quietly up to bed. Tomorrow you can tell us all about the party."

Laura started upstairs; then she stopped.

"Oh, Ma," she couldn't help saying, "each one of us had a whole orange!"

But she saved the rest to tell them all together.

Now that the party was over, Laura only wished it had lasted longer.

CHAPTER 8

The Bobsled

The party had made everyone even more friendly. Now at recess and at noon, the boys and girls gathered together and talked and laughed.

Sometimes they had big snowball fights, girls against boys. When the teacher rang the bell, Laura and her friends would come back to class panting and laughing. They stamped the snow from their boots and shook it from their coats. They went to their seats warm and glowing and full of fresh air.

After Christmas, the boys brought their

Christmas sleds to school. There were no hills to slide down. The prairie was wide and flat. This year there were no blizzards to make big, hard snowdrifts, as there had been the winter before. So the boys pulled the girls across the snow on the sleds.

Then Cap and Ben built a bobsled. It was big enough for Laura and Minnie and Mary and Ida to crowd into. At recess, Laura and her friends went racing far out onto the prairie and back. At noontime, they sometimes went even farther.

Nellie Oleson always stayed indoors. She said that it wasn't proper for girls to play outside in the snow. She didn't want to hurt her fair skin or chap her hands in the cold.

But one day, she couldn't stand watching all the fun from the window any longer. She announced that she would go for a sled ride too.

The bobsled was not big enough for five. But the boys hated to leave any of the girls behind. Everyone pushed and pulled. The girls' feet stuck out from the sides. Their skirts had to be gathered in until their stockings showed above their boots. Finally, all five girls squeezed into the sled. Away they went, whooshing out onto the snowy prairie.

The cold wind blew hard against their faces. Laura and the other girls laughed and sang as they whipped across the snow. Then the boys swung in a great circle over the prairie. They began to run back toward the schoolhouse.

The sled flew faster and faster. The wind whipped harder and the girls laughed louder. The sled whisked past the schoolhouse.

"Let's go up and down Main Street!" Cap teased. He knew the girls would be embarrassed to be seen on Main Street all squeezed into the little bobsled.

"Yes! Yes!" the other boys yelled, and they started running even faster.

"Oh, boys, you mustn't!" Ida called. But she couldn't stop laughing.

Laura was laughing, too. The girls were such a funny sight. Their heels were kicking helplessly. Their hair had come undone and their skirts and scarves were blowing in the wind.

Nellie was not laughing. She did not want to be seen on Main Street looking so unladylike.

"Stop this minute!" she cried. "Stop! Stop, I tell you!"

The boys didn't listen. Nellie began to scream, but it only made the boys go faster.

The bobsled was getting closer to town every second.

Laura was still laughing. She didn't think the boys would really take them down Main Street. She didn't mind looking funny with all her friends. But she didn't want everyone in town to see them. She felt sure the boys would stop any minute and turn back toward school.

But the sled kept heading straight for town.

Now Minnie began to scream. "No! No! Arthur, no!" she cried.

"Don't!" Mary Power begged. "Oh please, don't!"

Just then, Laura caught sight of the hitching post at the edge of town. All of a sudden, she knew that the boys really did mean to take them into town. They would go shrieking past all the eyes on Main Street.

Now it was not funny at all.

The other girls were so loud, Laura knew she had to speak low to be heard.

"Cap!" she said. "Please make them stop. Mary doesn't want to go on Main Street."

Cap heard Laura. He began to turn at once. The other boys pulled against him, but Cap said, "Aw, come on," and swung the sled around.

Now they were sailing toward the schoolhouse. The bell was ringing.

At the schoolhouse door, all the girls scrambled out of the sled. They shook the snow from their clothes.

Nellie was so angry, she could hardly speak.

"You—you—you *dumb westerners*!" Nellie cried.

The boys looked at Nellie and became

69

silent. They could not say what they wanted to because she was a girl. Then Cap glanced at Mary Power to see if she was as upset as Nellie. But Mary smiled at Cap.

"Thank you for the ride," Laura said then. She was not mad. She had loved riding fast across the snow. She was happy that the boys had not taken them into town. And so were the other girls.

"Yes, thank you all. It was such fun!" Ida chimed in.

"Thank you," Mary Power said.

Cap's big grin lit up his whole face.

"We'll go again at recess," he promised.

All the girls except for Nellie nodded their heads. Together the boys and girls went tromping through the schoolhouse door.

Laura took her seat next to Ida. Her face glowed from the cold and her eyes shone. It felt good to be a town girl and have so many friends.

LAURA INGALLS WILDER was born in 1867 in the log cabin described in LITTLE HOUSE IN THE BIG WOODS. As her classic Little House books tell us, she and her family traveled by covered wagon across the Midwest. She and her husband, Almanzo Wilder, made their own covered-wagon trip with their daughter, Rose, to Mansfield, Missouri. There Laura wrote her story in the Little House books and lived until she was ninety years old. For millions of readers, however, she lives forever as the little pioneer girl in the beloved Little House books.

RENÉE GRAEF received her bachelor's degree in art from the University of Wisconsin at Madison. She is the illustrator of the Kirsten books in the American Girls Collection, as well as numerous titles in the new Little House publishing program. She lives in Cedarburg, Wisconsin, with her husband, Tim, and their children, Maggie and Maxfield.

The LAURA *Years*
By Laura Ingalls Wilder
Illustrated by Garth Williams

The ROSE *Years*
By Roger Lea MacBride
**Illustrated by Dan Andreasen
& David Gilleece**

The CAROLINE *Years*
By Maria D. Wilkes
Illustrated by Dan Andreasen
